Young Cousins Mysteries

The Birthday Present Mystery

by Elspeth Campbell Murphy

Illustrated by Nancy Munger

Timothy   Sarah-Jane   Titus

*Everything good comes from God,
and every perfect gift is from him.*

James 1:17a (ICB)

BETHANY BACKYARD®
MINNEAPOLIS, MN 55438

Published by Bethany House Publishers
A Ministry of Bethany Fellowship International
11400 Hampshire Avenue South
Bloomington, Minnesota 55438
www.bethanyhouse.com

Printed in China

Library of Congress Cataloging-in-Publication Data

Murphy, Elspeth Campbell.
  The birthday present mystery / by Elspeth Campbell Murphy;
illustrated by Nancy Munger.
       p. cm. — (Young cousins mysteries; 1)
Summary: Sara-Jane and her cousins, Titus and Timothy, go to their neighbor's
birthday party and help him discover what his real present is.
  ISBN 0-7642-2494-8 (pbk.)
  [1. Cousins--Fiction. 2. Birthdays—Fiction. 3. Mystery and detective
stories.] I. Munger, Nancy, ill. II. Title.
  PZ7.M95316 Bi 2001
  [Fic]—dc21
                                                        2001002769

ISBN 0-7642-2494-8

Contents

1. The Gorilla at the Door   5

2. Who's Sam?   11

3. The Birthday Party   17

4. The Mysterious Present   23

5. The Best Present   29

Chapter One
The Gorilla at the Door

"S-J! Come here quick!"
said Sarah-Jane's cousin Titus.

"There's a gorilla
coming up your front walk!"

"That's nice," said Sarah-Jane.

"Look!" said Titus. "Look! *Look!*"

Sarah-Jane did not look up
from her mystery book.

She was always getting teased
about her wild imagination.

But nothing mysterious
ever happened around there.

So she was not going to fall
for some silly gorilla story.
No way. No how.

Her other cousin, Timothy,
ran to the window.

"S-J!" he said. "Look!
The gorilla has a bunch of balloons!
And a present!"

"That's nice," said Sarah-Jane.

Just then the doorbell rang.

"He's here! He's here!"

cried Timothy and Titus together.

"S-J! Do something! *Do* something!"

Sarah-Jane sighed and put down her book.

Someone was at the door.

She had better see who it was.

Sarah-Jane opened the door.

There was a gorilla
standing on her front porch.
He was holding a present
and a bunch of balloons.
And right away the gorilla began
to sing:

"Happy Birthday to you!
Happy Birthday to you!
Happy Birthday, dear Sam!
Happy Birthday to you!"

From the sound of the voice,
Sarah-Jane could tell it was a lady gorilla.
How nice!
A lady gorilla was singing to her!

"Uh…S-J," said Titus.

"It's not your birthday."

"And you're not Sam," said Timothy.

Chapter Two
Who's Sam?

"Oh, dear!" said the gorilla.
"Are you sure you're not Sam?
Maybe short for Samantha?"

"She's positive,"
said Timothy and Titus together.

"Her name is Sarah-Jane.
And we're her cousins,
Timothy and Titus.
No one named Sam lives here."

Sarah-Jane just shrugged.
She was looking at the present.

It was a big box.

And it looked kind of heavy.

"Then I must have the wrong house!"
said the gorilla.
"It's my first day on the job.
My name is Liz, by the way.
Here—hold these a minute, would you?"

She set the present on the porch
and handed the balloons to Sarah-Jane.

She pulled off her gorilla head
and handed it to Timothy.

She pulled off her gorilla hands
and handed them to Titus.

Then Liz the gorilla
dug around in her pockets
until she found a slip of paper.

"I'm supposed to be
at the house next door!" said Liz.

Sarah-Jane said,
"The only person who lives next door
is a nice old man named Mr. Green."

"Is his first name Sam?" asked Liz.

"I don't know," said Sarah-Jane.

"Well, I guess there's only one way
to find out," said Liz.

"I'll go over there and sing the song and see what happens."

She sounded worried about messing up again.

So Sarah-Jane said, "We'll go with you."

Sure, she wanted to help Liz out.... But she also wanted to see what was in that box!

At first they thought no one was home at the house next door.

But then they heard voices coming from the backyard.

So they went back there.

And sure enough,
they saw a birthday cake and balloons.
Old Mr. Green was having a party.
A banner said *HAPPY BIRTHDAY, SAM!*
They had come to the right place.

Chapter Three
The Birthday Party

Mr. Green and his friends looked up
when Liz and the cousins
came into the yard and Liz sang:

"Happy Birthday to you,
Happy Birthday to you,
Happy Birthday, dear Sam,
Happy Birthday to you."

"That's odd," Sarah-Jane whispered
to Timothy and Titus.
"What's odd?" they whispered back.
"No one looks surprised,"
said Sarah-Jane.

"Mr. Green looks surprised," said Titus.

"Yes," agreed Sarah-Jane.

"*Mr. Green* looks surprised.

But no one *else* does.

Don't you think that's odd?"

Before the boys could answer,

Mr. Green invited them to have some cake

and to look at his birthday presents.

The cake was *excellent*.

But the presents were, well…
bor-ing!

A pair of black socks.

A box of white handkerchiefs.

A book of stamps.

A jar of jam.

The cousins were too polite to say so,
but these were the most BORING presents
they had ever seen.

Maybe the gorilla's present
would be better.

"Aren't you going to open
your new present, Sam?"
Mr. Green's friends asked him.

"Oh, yes!" said Mr. Green.
Then he said, "That's odd!"

"What's odd?" asked the cousins.

"There's no tag on this present,"
said Mr. Green.

"I wonder who sent it.
It's very mysterious."

"We thought you liked mysteries,"
said one of his friends.

"I *do* like mysteries," said Mr. Green.
"I like *solving* them.
So let's see what's in this box!"

He opened the box,
and the cousins crowded around
to get a look.

The box was full of...
newspapers.

Chapter Four
The Mysterious Present

Newspapers?

"Dig down a little deeper,"
said Sarah-Jane.

"Maybe someone put a *little* present
in a great, big box.
That happens sometimes."

So Mr. Green dug down deeper.
The cousins helped him.
They liked solving mysteries, too.

But there was nothing in the box
except...newspapers.

"This is the most mysterious present
I ever got," said Mr. Green.

"We thought you liked mysteries,"
said another of his friends.

"I do," said Mr. Green.
"But this is a *very* odd present!"

"Well, then," said his friend.
"What was the *best* present you ever
got?"

"That's easy!" said Mr. Green.
"When I was eight years old,
my mother and father gave me a puppy."

"You should get a dog, Mr. Green,"
said Sarah-Jane.

She was thinking about how much fun
it would be to live next door to a puppy.

"I know I've been thinking about it
a lot lately," said Mr. Green.

Titus looked puzzled and asked,
"But don't you already have a dog?"
"No," said Mr. Green.
"What makes you say that?"
"This," said Titus.
He picked up something from the
flower bed.
It was a dog's chew toy.

"Now, how did *that* get there?"
asked Mr. Green.

"Maybe some stray dog
brought it into your yard and dropped it,"
said Timothy.

"Maybe," said Sarah-Jane.
"Except...this chew toy looks brand new.
There are no teeth marks on it at all."

She turned around to ask Liz
what she thought.

But Liz was gone.

Chapter Five
The Best Present

"Where did Liz go?" asked Sarah-Jane.

"She can't have gone far," said Timothy. "She forgot her head."

"She came here in a van," said Titus. "Is the van still here?"

The cousins went out front to check.

Yes, the van was still there.

And there was Liz—getting something out of the back of the van.

The cousins went over to see what was up.

"Hi!" said Liz. "I guess it's time for the second present now."

"*Second* present?" asked Timothy.

"Yes," said Liz.

"I was told to bring the box in first.
Then I was supposed to bring...this!"

"Oh!" gasped Sarah-Jane.

"He's the *perfect* present for Mr. Green!
And I think I know who sent him."

Sarah-Jane went back to Mr. Green
and said, "Your friends knew you like dogs.
And they knew you like mysteries.
So they wanted to give you a dog
for your birthday.
And they wanted to be mysterious about it.
That's why they sent you some clues."

"The chew toy!" said Timothy.

"And the newspapers!" said Titus.

"So the puppy doesn't mess up the floor."

"Of course!" said Mr. Green.

"But what about my other presents?"

His friends laughed.

"Those are not your *real* presents.
They're too boring.
The *puppy* is your real present."

Sarah-Jane said,
"I thought nothing mysterious
ever happened around here.
But with friends like yours…"

"My pals," agreed Mr. Green happily.

"Pal," said Sarah-Jane slowly.
"That might be a good name for…"

"…a puppy!" said Mr. Green. "Pal it is!
More cake, anyone?"

The End